Sidikiba's Kora Lesson

WRITTEN AND ILLUSTRATED BY

Ryan Thomas Skinner

SIDIKIBA'S KORA LESSON

© 2008 RYAN THOMAS SKINNER • MUSIC © 2008 SIDIKI DIABATÉ

ISBN 13: 978-1-59298-242-4
ISBN 10: 1-59298-242-5

LIBRARY OF CONGRESS CATALOG NUMBER: 2008937062

BOOK DESIGN AND LAYOUT: RICK KORAB, PUNCH DESIGN, INC. (WWW.PUNCH-DESIGN.COM)
AUDIO RECORDING AND MASTERING: KONAN KOUASSI, STUDIO MALI (BAMAKO, MALI)

PRINTED IN THE UNITED STATES OF AMERICA

FIRST PRINTING: 2008

12 11 10 09 08   5 4 3 2 1

Beaver's Pond Press

7104 OHMS LANE, SUITE 101
EDINA, MINNESOTA 55439 USA
(952) 829-8818
WWW.BEAVERSPONDPRESS.COM

TO ORDER, VISIT WWW.BOOKHOUSEFULFILLMENT.COM OR CALL 1-800-901-3480. RESELLER AND SPECIAL SALES DISCOUNTS AVAILABLE.

P R E F A C E

The **kora*** is a twenty-one stringed harp played by the Mande people of West Africa. Its round body is made of a large **calabash gourd** that is dried, cut in half, and covered with cow skin. Holes are cut into this drum-like body to allow insertion of a long wooden neck, handles, and support dowel. A block of wood covered in a red cotton cloth is placed on the flat face of the kora's body to support an ornamented wooden bridge. The nylon strings of the kora descend from twenty-one leather rings attached to the neck. They connect to the bridge with eleven strings on the left-hand side and ten on the right. The strings are tied to an iron ring that is fastened to the neck where it extends from the base of the kora. A hole is cut into the right-hand side of the body for sound to escape, and the kora's body is decorated with metal tacks according to the maker's taste and style.

terms in bold appear in the glossary at the back of the book

It is believed that the kora originated in the **Kaabu** empire that was founded in the modern-day country of Guinea-Bissau. According to Mande legend, a bard and storyteller named **Jeli Mady Wuleng** discovered the kora guarded by a female spirit in a cave outside of **Kansala**, the capital of Kaabu. He received the kora as a gift from the spirit and set about learning how to play it. He then composed the first kora song in honor of **Kelefa Sane**, one of Kaabu's greatest generals. As time went on, knowledge of the kora was passed down from one generation of musicians to another. When the bards traveled they brought their koras with them and shared its music and story with others.

The kora can now be found outside of Kaabu in countries such as Mali, The Gambia, Senegal, and Guinea. **Mali** is the traditional homeland of the Mande people. In its modern day capital, **Bamako**, lives **Sidikiba,** a young descendant of Jeli Mady Wuleng and heir to the knowledge and secrets of the kora. This is Sidikiba's story.

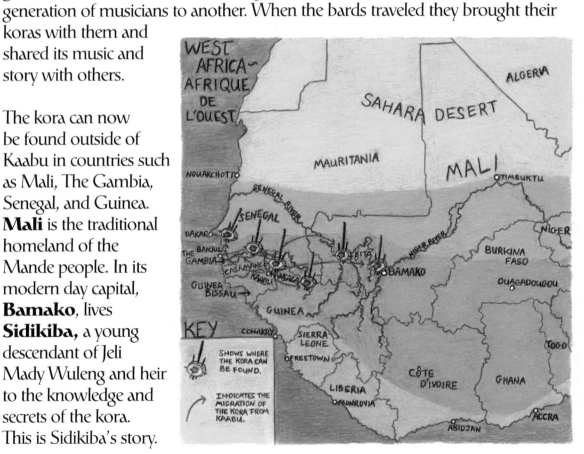

DEDICATIONS

To Toumani,

who initiated me into

the world of the kora,

and to Dialy Mady,

who taught me to live in it.

Sidikiba's Kora Lesson

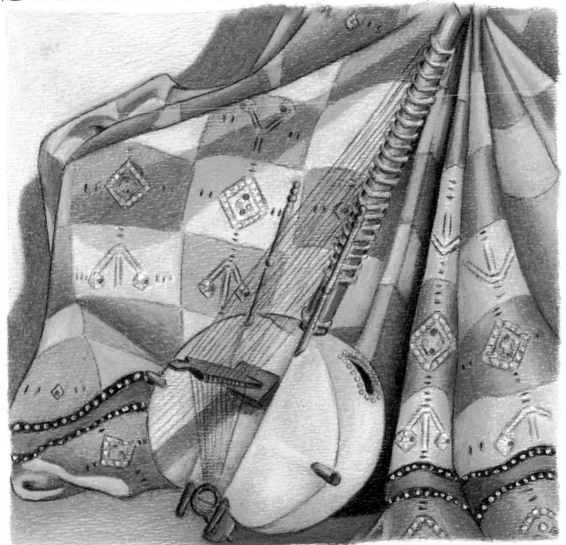

WRITTEN AND ILLUSTRATED BY RYAN THOMAS SKINNER

Sidikiba lives in a town on the outskirts of Bamako. Sidikiba is ten years old and the eldest of three children. Like most ten year-olds, Sidikiba attends primary school and enjoys playing with his friends. He likes soda pop and delights in being outside where his curiosity and imagination are free to explore. Sidikiba has not yet begun playing the kora. Even so, he is proud to be part of such a long line of kora players, and he often dreams of the day when he will learn to play just like his father and his grandfather before him.

He is proud to be part

of such a long line

of kora players

Sidikiba lives in a modern African house built of concrete and stone with a sturdy aluminum roof. It is colored with reddish-brown clay and layers of golden paint. He lives with his mother and father, brother and sister, uncles and aunts, cousins, grandmothers, and grandfathers. The house encompasses a large, open courtyard where nearly all of the family's daily activities and chores take place. A mango tree grows in the middle of the courtyard, its large oval leaves providing ample shade from the sweltering heat of the afternoon sun. In the late morning, clothes swing gently in the breeze as they dry under the warm rays of the sun, and the courtyard enjoys a moment of stillness before the family returns from the day's errands.

The house

encompasses a

large, open courtyard

One such morning, Sidikiba found himself reading quietly in the room he shared with his brother, Balla, and his sister, Jelika. Family members were gathering outside, and the familiar sounds of twigs snapping under children's feet, teapots whistling, and people talking loudly echoed through the room. Sidikiba frowned at these distractions and attempted to ignore them by focusing his gaze on his French grammar book. Sidikiba was eager to improve his French, Mali's official language, so he took his lessons quite seriously. On that particular day, however, the noises in the courtyard made it impossible for him to concentrate, so he left his room and went outside to see what all the commotion was about.

Sidikiba was eager to improve his French, Mali's official language

7

Sidikiba's irritation quickly faded when he saw the reason for the morning's disturbances. Sidikiba's father had returned home surrounded by a group of his friends, all adorned in colorful **boubous**. From a distance, Sidikiba listened to the jokes and laughter the group of jovial men exchanged.

"Eh! Mon ami! When are you going to play your kora for us? We didn't come all this way simply to drink your tea and eat your food! If you don't play we might spread rumors that Mali's greatest kora player has lost his touch!" one of the friends shouted. Sounds of agreement and laughter echoed from the others.

"Oh, and I am to believe that you have come here only to be entertained?" Sidikiba's father said with a wry smile. "You must be tired if you've traveled so far. Please, sit down and have some tea, then you may spread your rumors!" While he spoke, however, Sidikiba's father signaled to Sidikiba to bring his kora and seated himself in the shade of the mango tree.

Sidikiba's father had returned home surrounded by a group of his friends

Sidikiba's father received his kora with a smile. The base of the instrument dug into the gravel and soil, where it rested at an angle between his legs. He leaned in with his broad shoulders, held the kora gently with his strong hands, and set about tuning the magnificent instrument. His fingers danced gracefully over the kora's twenty-one strings and occasionally shifted a leather ring on the instrument's long neck. Then, he subtly introduced a delicate melody from his palette of notes. This melody soon became a song and suddenly the shrill, sweet sounds of women's voices sang brilliantly with the father's tune, "**Kayira**." Sidikiba's father had developed an esteemed reputation in Mali for being an exceptional kora player. While he played, his family and friends looked on with wonder as he improvised new melodies into this well-known piece. Sidikiba hid himself behind his grandmother's stout figure, watching and listening with astonishment as his father played.

(track 1)

His fingers danced gracefully over the kora's twenty-one strings

Sidikiba's father ended the song, received the compliments and thanks of his guests, and nodded at Sidikiba to return the kora to its case. The guests departed as cheerfully as they had arrived, and the family returned to their conversations, tea, and household chores. Sidikiba came back to his father carrying a smaller kora, and curiously asked, "Father, who does this kora belong to? I haven't seen it here before."

His father chuckled. "So Sidikiba, you have found your kora!"

"My kora?" Sidikiba asked, surprised. "But, but I don't have…I don't even know how to play it!" Sidikiba was bewildered and somewhat nervous.

His father responded solemnly, "Go and speak with your uncle, Jeli Mady. He made this kora for you and will tell you what you must do next. It's time for you to learn to play the kora, Sidikiba." He placed his hand on Sidikiba's shoulder and smiled.

Hesitantly, Sidikiba took his new kora, admired its fine craftsmanship, and nodded silently in appreciation. He was both confused and excited by what had transpired that morning. He left to see his uncle unaware of his mother's prideful gaze.

It's time for you to learn to play the kora

Jeli Mady was actually Sidikiba's father's cousin, but Sidikiba knew him as "uncle" because of the close relationship Jeli Mady and Sidikiba's father had shared over the years. Jeli Mady lived with his own family in a neighboring house and inhabited a room that served both as his bedroom and his workshop. Like Sidikiba's father, Jeli Mady was also a skilled kora player, but he had always preferred to make the instruments and was well respected for his trade. Jeli Mady had also acquired knowledge of many of the kora's secrets, and was well versed in the old traditions associated with the instrument. Without any children of his own, Jeli Mady held a certain fondness for Sidikiba and desired greatly to pass on his knowledge of the kora to him. The day Sidikiba arrived with his new kora, Jeli Mady was expecting him.

Jeli Mady had also acquired knowledge of many of the kora's secrets

Sidikiba hastily entered Jeli Mady's room and greeted him with excitement. He clumsily propped his kora in an empty corner of the room and sprang into his uncle's lap with a beaming smile.

"You know you should be more careful with your new instrument, Sidikiba. The kora is like a human being. You must learn to treat it with respect," Jeli Mady said with raised eyebrows and a slight grin.

Sidikiba blushed, jumbling his words as he spoke, "Well, I . . . I just wanted to see you, or father said to see you, and I didn't mean to, it's just that . . . sorry."

Jeli Mady laughed. "Well, I will forgive you this time, but next time remember what you have been told. Here, I have something for you." Jeli Mady reached into his cupboard and removed a brown paper bag.

"What is it, uncle?" Sidikiba asked as he stared at the mysterious bag.

His uncle grinned and said, "In this bag there are ten **kola nuts**. You must take these as an offering to your grandfather before you may begin playing your kora."

Sidikiba took the bag, thanked his uncle sincerely, and left the room carrying both his kora and the ten kola nuts, feeling excited by the day's unusual turn of events.

17

Sidikiba returned home and found his grandfather playing his old kora on the wooden bench outside his room in the courtyard. Sidikiba's grandfather was a clever and comical old man with a profound respect for tradition and a gift for storytelling. Children from all around the village often came to sit and listen to Sidikiba's grandfather tell his colorful stories. With his clear, sharp voice and flawless kora playing, Sidikiba's grandfather told of the great exploits of the old kings of Mali, the struggles and sorrows of famous battles, and the renowned generosity of stately Malian patrons. Sidikiba particularly enjoyed it when his grandfather recounted his own long and difficult journey from The Gambia to Mali, made on foot when he was still a young man. Sidikiba was very fond of his grandfather and often went to him for consolation when he felt troubled or sad. When Sidikiba arrived to deliver the ten kola nuts that his uncle had given him, he paused for a moment to listen to his grandfather perform the prelude to Mali's greatest epic, "**Sunjata**," the story of the founding of Old Mali.

(track 2)

Sidikiba's grandfather told of the great exploits of the old kings of Mali

18

till playing his kora, Sidikiba's grandfather carefully eyed his grandson and noticed with interest the brown paper bag he held in his lap.

"What is it that brings you here on this fine day my dear boy? Shouldn't you be out playing with your friends?" he inquired. His lingering gaze revealed his true interest in the sack that Sidikiba nervously crumpled in his hands.

Sidikiba smiled at his grandfather and said, "I have just come from my uncle, Jeli Mady, and I have brought you a gift." Sidikiba then opened the bag and presented the ten kola nuts that lay inside. His grandfather calmly ended his kora performance and set aside his instrument.

Taking the bag of kola nuts, the grandfather gently nodded his head and spoke solemnly, "What you have done is good and shows your desire to bind yourself with the kora, our family's instrument for seventy generations. Is that what you wish to do?"

Sidikiba was unaccustomed to his grandfather's serious tone, Sidikiba responded timidly, "Yes, grandfather, I . . . I want to learn to play the kora, like you and father."

His grandfather smiled and took Sidikiba's hands in his own, bowed his head and began to utter a traditional prayer with words that Sidikiba could scarcely hear.

When the ceremonial prayer had ended, Sidikiba's grandfather took up his kora and began to play. Sidikiba stared intently at his grandfather's skillful fingers as they plucked and strummed the strings of the kora. The song was different from the one his grandfather had been playing before, and to Sidikiba's surprise he did not recognize it!

With his eyes closed, Sidikiba's grandfather took in a deep breath and spoke, "Listen carefully, my son. This is the song for Kelefa Sane, who was one of Kaabu's bravest and most cunning warriors. This song was composed long ago by your ancestor, Jeli Mady Wuleng, and is the first song that was ever composed for the kora. "Kelefaba" is to be learned by all kora students at their initiation."

(track 3)

Sidikiba's grandfather did not wait for a response from his grandson and continued to play. The rhythm of his performance accelerated and the accompanying melodies he played became more and more complex, running up and down the kora's scale, touching every string. The song went on and on but neither Sidikiba nor his grandfather took notice. Finally, as the afternoon sun hung low over the horizon, the grandfather ended the song and said softly, "Now, Sidikiba, go and practice what you have learned."

That evening, as shadows crept over the walls of the courtyard, Sidikiba set about learning "Kelefaba." Sidikiba placed the kora down between his legs, took hold of the handles with a light, yet supportive grip, and attempted to move his index fingers and thumbs over the kora's strings as his grandfather had done. Unfortunately, the jarring and dissonant noises his kora produced sounded nothing like the clean, fluid melodies his grandfather had played. Sidikiba's first thought was that his kora must be flawed in some way, but when he looked at it more carefully he found nothing wrong. "It's only me and my clumsy fingers that don't work!" he thought to himself angrily. "This is our family's instrument, and I can't play a single note right! Perhaps the kora is just not meant for me." He left his kora in the courtyard and went to his room to study his French lessons. Sidikiba did not want to think about the kora or his initiation any longer, but the feeling of shame lingered inside him as he imagined his father's disappointment at his failure.

Sidikiba did not want to think about the kora or his initiation any longer

When Sidikiba returned home from school the next day, he found his uncle, Jeli Mady, awaiting expectantly for him in the courtyard. Jeli Mady held Sidikiba's kora firmly between his legs while alternately plucking strings, listening, and shifting the leather rings on the neck.

When Jeli Mady saw Sidikiba called to him, "Well, if it isn't the new kora student! Come here and I will show you how to tune your instrument!"

Remembering his failure the evening before, Sidikiba reluctantly greeted him. "Uncle, maybe it's not such a great idea for me to learn the kora right now. I mean, maybe I'm still too young."

"Nonsense!" his uncle said, "There are many boys your age who are already learning to play the kora. Now watch carefully!" Jeli Mady then demonstrated how to tune the strings by raising and lowering the leather rings on the kora's neck. "Here, now you try."

Sidikiba slowly played through the kora's scale, noticed a note that didn't seem to sound right, and, with a bit of effort, adjusted the ring until the string was in harmony with the others. Sidikiba was amazed, and although he still could not play the song his grandfather had shown him, he was happy to know that it was his kora, not him, that needed adjusting!

Under his uncle's tutelage Sidikiba finally began to understand the basic melody of "Kelefaba," his first song. Pleased with his nephew's progress, Jeli Mady introduced new melodies for Sidikiba to practice, and they played and played until Sidikiba's fingers grew heavy with fatigue.

"Very good!" Jeli Mady exclaimed, "Now, there is one more thing I want to show you this evening, but we must hurry if we are to get there on time!" Jeli Mady then set Sidikiba's kora aside and told him to find a strong rope.

Confused Sidikiba asked, "But, uncle, I don't quite understand. Why do we need a rope? Where are we going?"

"No time for questions!" Jeli Mady bellowed. "Quickly! There's no time to lose!"

They left the house and began to walk hastily toward the village market. Jeli Mady whistled a tune as he set the pace with long, confident steps. Sidikiba scurried along behind him alternating between quick steps and a light jog. When they arrived at the marketplace Jeli Mady approached a table occupied by a short, amiable market-woman. He placed his order, articulating each syllable as he spoke, "One pure white hen, and a young male goat with a light brown face, please." They negotiated a reasonable price and the animals were brought out.

Sidikiba, whose rope was now tied around the surly goat's neck, looked on with excitement and apprehension.

They left the marketplace with their animals and emerged onto the dusty road that led to the end of town. Jeli Mady said they were to see a friend of his in a nearby village. "We must hurry," he urged, "because he closes his doors at sundown."

"But, uncle, who is this friend of yours? What does he do?" Sidikiba asked as he strained to pull the stubborn goat along.

"He is a **marabout**," his uncle replied, "a traditional soothsayer who can offer you guidance and a glimpse into your future. Many kora students have gone to seek his council. I myself have spoken with him several times!"

"A marabout!" Sidikiba thought to himself with excitement. Sidikiba had often wondered what a marabout's house would look like. His step quickened despite the obstinacy of his four-legged companion.

They arrived as the sun's final rays cast long shadows over the flat and dry landscape. A sign read "TRADITIONAL HEALER" above the open doorway that was concealed by a thick curtain. Inside they found the marabout sitting upon layers of floor matting and pelts. His dimly lit room was littered with open bags, colorful glass bottles and jars, books of all kinds, used candles, and melted wax. On his walls hung carved amulets, leather belts, beaded necklaces, cotton robes, and vivid tapestries. Sidikiba couldn't believe his eyes. It was all just as he had imagined!

I nside the room, Jeli Mady exchanged greetings with his friend and sat down beside him on the straw mat. Sidikiba remained within the arch of the doorway, the goat lying indifferently beside him.

"And this is my nephew, Sidikiba!" Jeli Mady proudly announced, pointing toward the door. "He is learning to play the kora, so we have brought you this hen and this goat as offerings for a glimpse into his future."

"To learn the kora and discover its secrets is to embark on a long and difficult journey," the marabout said gravely. "Come closer, my boy, and we will see where your path shall lead."

Sidikiba cautiously approached the two men and knelt down behind them. The marabout picked up a green piece of chalk and drew a series of long and short lines on the ruddy clay floor. He erased this first set of lines, grumbled, and produced a new series. These too he erased. He repeated the process several times until he uttered a satisfied grunt and set his chalk on the ground.

He spoke, "Sidikiba, your future is bright and shows potential for great success, but fortune does not come to the lazy. You must honor the kora and remain loyal to your studies. To help you I will give you a small charm wrapped in leather that you must place secretly inside your kora. This will bring you good luck."

Sidikiba and Jeli Mady thanked the soothsayer and got up to leave. On the road home Sidikiba stared up at the vast array of stars in the night sky and held his amulet tightly in his hand.

Days and weeks went by, and Sidikiba continued to play his kora and practice the melodies he had learned, never forgetting his puzzling encounter with the marabout. Sidikiba had not yet given a performance with his kora and shied away from any suggestions for him to do so, especially those that came from his family.

Late one morning, Sidikiba was home from school throwing marbles with his brother and sister when he heard the playful sounds of string music coming from the courtyard. He gathered his marbles and those he had won from his siblings and went outside to see who was playing. He saw that it was his cousin, Amadu, playing his kora with a friend who strummed and tapped a rather large **ngoni** lute. Sidikiba listened closely to their song, accompanying them softly with a melodic hum. He recognized the tune as "**Kanu**," a touching love song that Sidikiba's mother had often sung for him and his siblings when they were younger.

(track 4)

After finishing their song, Sidikiba ran into his room, ignoring the protests of his brother and sister whose game he disturbed. He took his kora and hurried toward the doorway, carefully avoiding the scattered marbles as he left.

When Sidikiba arrived he found Amadu tuning his kora in the shade of the mango tree. Amadu's friend had left, so Sidikiba sat in the chair next to his cousin. Sidikiba greeted Amadu warmly and complimented him on his performance.

"Thank you, Sidikiba!" Amadu said, smiling. "We're thinking of forming a group, but we're both so busy and there is still so much to rehearse!" Noticing the kora Sidikiba held in front of him, he added, "So, it's true what the family's been saying, you have begun to learn the kora!"

"Can you teach me a song?" Sidikiba appealled as he adjusted the leather rings of his kora.

"Well, I suppose I can, if you feel up to it!" said Amadu. "Let's try '**Mali Cajo**.' It's about an old hippopotamous who lived peacefully among humans all his life." He closed his eyes and began to play.

(track 5)

Sidikiba watched his cousin's fingers carefully and followed their movements as best he could on his own kora. Sweat began to bead on Sidikiba's forehead as he concentrated on his thumbs and index fingers. Then the song became even faster and more complex! Sidikiba once again looked at Amadu's hands in an attempt to orient himself but instead stopped playing altogether when he saw the rapid blur of Amadu's fingers dancing along the kora's stings.

36

Sidikiba gently laid his kora down and drew closer to Amadu whose fingers moved steadily through the wave of notes that flowed from his kora. Earlier, he believed that he had made considerable progress in his study of the kora, but now, as he watched his cousin play, he understood how much he still had to learn. Despite this, Sidikiba remained hopeful.

Amadu abruptly sent a series of notes cascading down the strings of the kora, dramatically ending this rare and extraordinary recital. "Sorry." He said breathlessly, exhausted by the performance. "Sometimes I get a bit carried away!"

"That was… *incredible!*" Sidikiba exclaimed. "I… I can't believe it! How did you learn to play so fast?" He examined Amadu's kora, searching for an explanation for what he had just witnessed, but he found nothing unusual.

"Sidikiba, behind every skill there are two things: practice, and a good secret! Come with me, and I'll show you mine." Sidikiba agreed, and they left to see Amadu's grandfather, **Nfa**.

Behind every skill there are two things: practice, and a good secret!

Amadu's grandfather was known to everybody in their village as "Nfa", which in the Bamana language means "my father." This title began with his own children who never called him by any other name, and it was soon generally accepted by local villagers that Nfa was their father too. Nfa lived with his children and grandchildren in an old concrete house near the town marketplace. He was a quiet, simple man, spending most of his time in his cluttered workshop at home building koras. His modest disposition, however, enhanced his reputation as an exceptionally wise town elder. He was also said to be an expert kora player, although he rarely played the instrument he was so fond of making. In fact, it was only when he had finished building a kora that he desired to play it.

Sidikiba and Amadu arrived at Nfa's workshop in the late morning, just in time for a fresh round of sweet green tea. Nfa was in the process of preparing the tuning rings for a new kora, so Amadu and Sidikiba offered their greetings and calmly waited while he finished measuring and cutting lengths of leather.

It was only when he had finished building a kora that he desired to play it

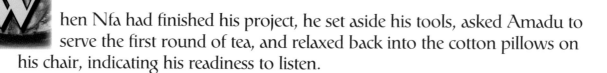

hen Nfa had finished his project, he set aside his tools, asked Amadu to serve the first round of tea, and relaxed back into the cotton pillows on his chair, indicating his readiness to listen.

Amadu spoke first. "Nfa, I have brought my cousin Sidikiba here today because he asked to know the secret of the kora player's quick and nimble fingers. We have come because you are the only kora player in the village who possesses this knowledge. He has been initiated, and I believe he is ready for the ceremony."

Sidikiba was confused by Amadu's language, and although he meant to ask what ceremony Amadu was referring to, he found he said "Yes, I am ready," instead.

Staring directly at Sidikiba through his thick, black-rimmed glasses, Nfa spoke, "This young boy is part of a long and great family of kora players. Seventy generations have gone before him. His eyes possess the fiery spirit of his father and the wisdom of his grandfather." Nfa then turned to Amadu and said, "Go and fetch the clay pot and fill it with hot coals, and bring the jar of incense from my cupboard."

Sidikiba was now more confused than ever. "What do hot coals and incense have to do with quick fingers?" he thought to himself.

Amadu brought the clay pot filled with red-hot coals and set it on the ground between his grandfather and Sidikiba. He then pulled out the small jar of incense from his pocket and opened it, filling the room with the fragrant smells of dried flowers, spices and oils. Nfa took the open jar and dropped three spoonfuls of incense onto the coals. The incense hissed as it slowly burned on the glowing embers, releasing a sweet, pungent smoke that gently rose out of the clay pot.

When he had finished the preparations, Nfa gave a wrinkled smile and said, "Now, young Sidikiba, you must place your hands in the smoke above the coals."

Sidikiba obeyed without uttering a single word. His confusion had faded away. As the ceremony began, he became calm and serious.

Nfa first muttered a series of old prayers calling for cleansing, healing, and renewal. He then took a cloth from his shirt pocket, dipped it in water, and used it to gently massage Sidikiba's fingers. When Nfa had finished, he carefully folded the cloth and returned it to his pocket. Next, he reached out with his hands to touch the twenty-one strings of a kora that stood beside him and then touched Sidikiba's hands. He moved between the kora's strings and Sidikiba's fingers again, and once more. After the third movement Nfa released Sidikiba's hands and allowed the dwindling smoke to curl through his fingers, saying, "Remove your hands from the smoke. It is over."

As time went on, Sidikiba became more and more devoted to his study of the kora. He paid attention to the songs his father and grandfather played and learned their stories. He grew out his fingernails, as he had seen other kora students do, so that he could better pluck and strum the strings. He could hear himself getting better, although he remained reluctant to play alone in front of others and was especially afraid to play for his father.

One day, in the late morning when the house was empty except for the children and their grandfather, who was still sleeping, Sidikiba took his kora out into the courtyard and began to practice. He played "**Allah Baara**," a song he had heard his father perform many times.

(track 6)

From inside their room Balla and Jelika heard the pleasing sounds of the kora and wondered who could be playing it. Quietly, they opened the door, looked at the figure in the shade of the mango tree, and saw that it was their brother! They ran to him with shouts of joy, shouting over and over again, "Sidikiba can play the kora!" This time their presence did not discourage Sidikiba, and he continued to play, allowing himself to improvise new melodies and complex rhythms.

idikiba's mother usually spent her mornings at the marketplace where the village women gathered to socialize, discuss their families, and purchase fresh fruits and vegetables. On the day that Sidikiba played his kora for his brother and sister, however, she stood in her room, preparing herself for a marriage ceremony she was to attend that afternoon. As she adorned herself in colorful fabrics and gold jewelry, she began to sing a familiar melody. While she sang, she believed she was imagining a kora playing along with her when, suddenly, she heard the delighted cries of her children outside. She swung open her door and was overwhelmed by what she saw. Balla and Jelika sang and danced happily around Sidikiba who confidently and skillfully played his kora under a canopy of leaves in the courtyard.

"Come and hear my son play the kora!" She exclaimed to whomever might be listening, "Sidikiba, you have made your mother proud today!"

In a full-throated and piercing voice, Sidikiba's mother began singing his praises and those of their family. Young Balla danced happily to these festive sounds, while Jelika, paying careful attention to her mother's song, began to sing and praise her brother. All the while, Sidikiba continued to play his kora.

Sidikiba's mother began singing his praises and those of their family

The morning's surprise became greater with the arrival of Sidikiba's father and Jeli Mady who returned to the house for a late breakfast. Sidikiba's father was deeply moved when he saw his family joyfully singing in praise of his elder son whose music he was hearing for the first time. The two men approached the circle of singing and dancing figures and greeted them warmly. Seeing his father, Sidikiba became awkward and nervous, lost his concentration, and abruptly ended his performance. Nonetheless, he received applause from the surrounding family.

"Sidikiba, you have come a long way in your studies of the kora, and I am very proud of you," his father said, seating himself beside his son. "Jeli Mady has told me of your adventures, and now I see that you have indeed learned your lessons well. I would only ask to hear one more melody this morning, 'Kelefaba,' the song all kora players must learn to play at their initiation."

(track 7)

Sidikiba nodded his head, took a deep breath, and stretched his fingers. As he played he thought of the kola nuts he had offered his grandfather and the charm that lay concealed in his kora. He believed he could feel the smoke of the incense still curling through his fingers as it had in Nfa's workshop. He played and played, and heard his father exclaim, "My son, the kora player! Tonight we shall celebrate!"

50

G L O S S A R Y

Allah Baara:　　A traditional song performed by West African bards meaning "God's Work" (pronounced: AH-lah BAH-rah).

Bamako:　　The capital city of Mali (pronounced: BAH-mah-KOH).

Boubou:　　A brightly colored, elaborately embroidered robe worn by men in West Africa. In Mali, it is often called a "long shirt." (pronounced: BOO-BOO).

Calabash Gourd:　　The large, spherical, and woody fruit of the tropical Calabash plant. The gourds are cleaned and dried and used for bowls, utensils, and musical instruments like the kora (pronounced: KA-lah-BASH).

Jeli:　　The Mande term for bard or storyteller (pronounced: JEH-lee). In West Africa, you are born a jeli. You do not become one. There are a dozen or so clans that consider themselves to be jelis in West Africa. "Jeli" is also a traditional title given to some people born into such clans, as in the name "Jeli Mady."

Jeli Mady Wuleng:　　The name of the first known kora player, according to oral history (pronounced: JEH-lee MAH-dee WOO-len).

Jembe:　　A West African hand drum (pronounced: JEM-bay).

Kaabu:　　A West African empire that existed from the mid-sixteenth century to the late-nineteenth century. It was located in present-day Guinea-Bissau (pronounced: KAH-boo).

Kansala:	The capital of the Kaabu empire. According to traditional accounts, the kora is said to originate in this city (pronounced: kahn-SAH-lah).
Kanu:	A traditional love lament performed by West African bards. The word "kanu" means "love" (pronounced: KAH-noo).
Kayira:	A popular song composed in the mid-twentieth century meaning "peace" (pronounced: KAYE-rah).
Kelefa Sane:	A warrior-prince of the Kaabu empire to whom the first known song composed for the kora, "Kelefaba," is dedicated (pronounced: KAY-LAY-fah SAH-nay).
Kola nut:	A large, bitter nut eaten throughout West Africa. The kola nut (pronounced: KOH-lah) has strong symbolic value in the region. In Mali, a man will give the family of his fiancée ten kola nuts before they marry. The same gesture applies to a young kora student who "gets engaged" to the instrument by offering the nuts to his mentor to become an apprentice.
Kora:	A twenty-one stringed West African harp performed by traditional Mande musicians (pronounced: KOH-rah).
Mali:	The name of an empire founded in the thirteenth century and lasting until the early seventeenth century. It is also the name of the modern West African Republic where this story takes place (pronounced: MAH-lee).

Mali Cajo: A traditional song from Western Mali that tells the story of a hippopotamus named Cajo (pronounced: CHAH-joh) after the animal's white speckled feet. The song pays tribute to Mali Cajo who lived in harmony with the people of a nearby village.

Mande: A cultural group with historical ties dating to the founding of the Mali empire in the thirteenth century (pronounced: MAHN-day). Currently Mande peoples live in countries such as: Mali, Mauritania, Senegal, The Gambia, Guinea Bissau, Sierra Leone, Guinea, Côte d'Ivoire, and Burkina Faso.

Marabout: A traditional, West African religious healer (pronounced: MAH-RAH-boo).

Nfa: Literally, a phrase, "n fa," meaning "my father" that is also an affectionate title for a respected elder (pronounced: in-FAH).

Ngoni: A traditional banjo-like lute with six to eight strings performed throughout West Africa and beyond (pronounced: in-GOH-nee).

Sidikiba: A name derived from the Arabic "Sadiq," meaning "friend," and the Mande suffix "ba," meaning "big" or "great" (pronounced: see-DEE-KEE-bah).

Sunjata: The legendary Mande hero who founded the Mali empire in the thirteenth century (pronounced: soon-JAH-tah).